Charlie and the Kitten

by

C.A. GOODY

illustrated by

TERRY LAAKER

Cover design by Reid Johns and Kim Hurley
Written and Printed in the U.S.A.
Typeset by TKPrinting
Printed by Central Plain Book Manufacturing

Copyright (c) 2006 by C.A. Goody

First Printing April 2006
ISBN 978-0-9702546-6-5

Goody, C.A. 1962-
Charlie's Great Adventure
Charlie Moves to Arizona
Charlie and the Rodent Queen
Charlie Goes Camping
Charlie and the Kitten

Summary - Charlie the cat and his kitten friend try to help a little boy.
1 - Animal Adventure   2 - Cats   3 - Humor   4 - Children

DEDICATIONS

To My Lord Jesus Christ,
who makes all things possible.

And to my best friend Fran; thank you for loving,
encouraging, and always being there for me.

TABLE OF CONTENTS

Chapter 1

A Strange Stranger

HAVE YOU ever noticed that every time life gets to be just the way you like it, just the way you pictured it should be, something happens to change things around?

I have. Life as a cat is terrific, at least for me. I have a wonderful home, a sweet little girl who loves me (Amanda), a great pal that happens to be a toddler (Andrew), and a mom and a dad who love and feed us all. There is also a dog in the family, who I consider to be a friend even though she's not very bright (Frisky), and a hamster that is a little bossy but is still fun to talk with (Rose). With a family like that, you would think things would be hectic and happy. And they were. Until someone else showed up and turned my world upside down.

I had no reason to be alarmed that day when the

knock sounded at the front door. People came to the door all the time: friends dropping by; drivers making deliveries; kids selling things; and people carrying bibles. It was nothing unusual. I wandered toward the sound of voices when I heard Mom talking, figuring that if it were someone I knew, I could rub against their legs and get some attention. But I was in for a horrible shock.

"It should only be for a couple of days," the woman was saying. I recognized her as one of Mom's friends. She looked upset and sounded as if she were trying not to cry. Just as I was beginning to wonder what was going on, the woman handed Mom a kitten.

Okay, I need to explain something here. Mom loves animals (especially me), and she takes great care of us. Over the last few months, there had been several times when Dad or one of the kids had talked about getting another pet, but Mom was very adamant, "NO." She always said that she had more than enough on her hands to take care of with two kids, a good sized dog, an overactive cat, and a hamster that thought she deserved royal treatment. She insisted that there would not be additional animals in the house for a long time to come.

So when the lady put the kitten in Mom's hands, I figured she was going to give it right back. And that would be a good thing. I am quite enough cat for one house, thank you very much. I don't need anyone else around challenging my authority or stealing any of my attention.

But she didn't hand it back. She just held on to it while talking softly to her friend. "It's no problem. Just let me know what's going on and if there's anything else we can do to help. Don't worry; everything will be all right...."

No, everything will not be all right. Not with another cat in the house!

The lady left, and Mom turned around, not really seeing anything. "Oh, my," I heard her say, and then she started praying under her breath.

I wasn't paying any attention. I was staring at the furry bundle huddled against her chest. The kitten was a small, orange and white striped tabby, with lots of fluffy fur. It had wide brown eyes that looked confused and a little scared. Then he looked down and spotted me.

He immediately turned into a big ball of fluff. His fur was sticking straight out in every direction, his back was arched almost into a circle, and he was spitting and hissing like he was having a fit.

Now, I'm a very easy going cat. I try to get along with everyone. But, when someone takes an aggressive stance like that, you have to be ready. I felt my back arch up and my fur rise. My ears went back and my claws seemed to jump right out of my paws. Still, I tried to keep my voice calm as I said, "What's your problem?"

I was curious about how he would respond to this. He could either calm down and realize that I wasn't attacking him, or he could freak out even more and try to jump me. What I wasn't expecting was for him to burst out laughing.

"You look like you have a Mohawk!" he squeaked between giggles.

"What?"

"Your fur," he continued between chuckles. "It's so short, except on your back. When you stand it up, you just have a black stripe running from head to tail! You look like a total punk rocker!"

He kept laughing and laughing. He finally ran out of breath and lay in Mom's arms, gasping for air. "Are you done?" I asked him.

He looked down at me. "Yeah, your hair is all smoothed out again, so it's not as funny anymore." He stared at me. "Wow, when you're not hunched up, you look really cool."

All right, I'm a sucker for compliments. I decided to forgive him for laughing at me. "I'm Charlie. What's your name?"

"I'm Rev," he said, like I should be impressed.

"What kind of a name is that?" I asked him.

Just then, Mom spoke up. "Thank you for being nice about this, Charlie. It looks like you've got the kitten calmed down already." She rubbed his ears as she spoke.

The kitten started purring. It was one of the loud-est sounds I had ever heard. Like a jet engine, or a speedboat, or a ... car engine revving up.

"Yup. That's were my name comes from," he said. I was surprised I could hear him over the roar.

Mom carried him into the living room and set him down on the couch. Then she turned around and started petting me. "Will you please show Rev around the house Charlie? He'll only be here for a few days. I'll make sure there's plenty of food set out for both of you."

"Meow," I answered. I figured that as long as I got my share of food and attention, I would be able to handle having a visitor for a short time.

Mom left the room, and the kitten began sniffing around. He jumped down from the couch and ran over to the corner of the room, where Andrew's blocks were all piled.

"What's that?" he asked.

"Those are some of Andrew's toys. He's a little

boy, and you'll probably meet him pretty soon," I answered.

He ran over to the TV stand. "What's that?"

"That's a TV."

"What's that?"

"That's the video game controller," I answered.

"What's that?"

"A remote control."

"What's that?"

"A stereo. It plays music," I answered.

"What's that?"

"What's that?"

"What's that?"

This went on until he had sniffed at, looked at, and poked at everything in the room. Suddenly the fur on his back stood up again. "What's that?!"

He seemed to be staring at a spot in the middle of the carpet with nothing on it. "What's what?" I asked.

"That smell! I've never smelled anything like that before," he said with a wild look in his eyes.

I walked over to where he was standing and took a whiff. At first, I didn't smell anything unusual, and then I realized what it was. "Do you know what a dog is?" I asked him carefully.

His eyes got even bigger. "My mom told me about those. They're big, and hairy, and they like to chase cats and bite them! They're clever, and they will trap you and then eat you!" By the time he finished saying this, he had scared himself so much that his whole body was one big ball of fluff.

"Okay, maybe some dogs are vicious and mean. Some of them may even be smart. However, the dog that lives here is none of those things. She's...."

"THERE"S A DOG WHO LIVES HERE?" he shouted. He ran over to the couch and smashed himself in behind it.

"It's okay," I said very calmly. "Frisky is not mean. She is not vicious, and she is NOT clever. She likes cats. She and I are friends, and I'll make sure she's nice and doesn't hurt you."

He crawled out from the tiny space. "You're friends with a dog?" he asked in an awed voice. "You must be the bravest cat in the whole world!"

Well, it wouldn't hurt anything for him to think that. After all, he was only going to be here for a few days, and maybe if he thought I was some kind of hero-cat, then he wouldn't be so frightened. "Let's go find some food," I said in a big-brotherly way.

"Yes! I'm starved!" he yelped. I would soon find out that he was always hungry.

I took him back to the small room where Mom kept my food dish and litter box. I noticed she had already set out a separate bowl for Rev. He again followed his nose toward the smell; this time at a dead run.

"What is this?" he said in a voice of wonderment. "It smells amazing!"

"It's cat food," I told him.

"No way! My cat food never smelled this good." He threw his face into the dish and began to chow down.

While he was eating...; did I say eating? It was more like he was inhaling his food. Picture a vacuum cleaner sucking up every last morsel without stopping. I swear I could actually see his stomach get bigger and rounder as he continued to scarf the meal. Anyway, while he devoured his lunch, Dad, Amanda, and Andrew came home. They had been at the park playing all afternoon. I heard them chattering and laughing as they came in the door, and then I heard Mom telling them that we had a visitor for a few days.

"We have to be very careful with him," I heard her saying. "He's just a baby, so he's fragile. Andrew, you have to be especially careful. You need to hold him as if you were holding eggs; gently. Remember that he's little and delicate."

I looked over at the fragile little baby. He had just finished eating the entire bowl full of cat food, and as he sat up, he let out a huge burp.

Delicate. Yeah, right.

Chapter 2

Charlie Save the Queen

I FOLLOWED Rev into the kitchen, shaking my head. Kittens.

"What's that smell?" he asked, with his nose in the air.

I took a whiff. "Uhg, dog food. Mom must have just filled Frisky's bowl."

Rev's nose led him to the dish in the corner. He looked at the round chunks all piled up inside. "It smells kinda good. Not as good as that cat food we ate, but still sorta yummy." He reached a paw inside the bowl and scooped out one chunk. As it hit the floor, it rolled a little, and suddenly his eyes lit up. He batted it with his paw, and then took off chasing it across the room.

"Dog food is the greatest toy ever!" he yelled as

he raced across the carpet, propelling the chunk of dog chow in front of him. When it hit the wall and couldn't go forward anymore, he picked it up in his mouth, carried it over about three feet, then set it down and whapped it with his paw again.

After about ten minutes of chasing it around the house, he began to tire. He picked up the piece of food in his mouth, carried it back to the kitchen, and dropped it into one of Andrew's shoes in the corner. "This way, no one else will find it," I heard him say to himself.

Why would anyone else want to?

Then he walked over to Frisky's bowl, squatted over the top of it, and peed in the bowl.

"What are you doing?" I shouted at him.

"If I do this, it won't smell so yummy, and the dog won't eat it. Then, I'll have lots of toys to play with all day long!"

I just stared at him. "Well, don't let Mom or Frisky catch you doing that," I told him. "Mom will yell and then lock you in with the litter-box for an hour. Frisky, on the other hand, will probably bite your head off."

His eyes got so big, they took up his whole face. "Are you serious?"

"I learned that lesson my very first day in this family. Never mess with a dog's food."

"Is it still okay if I play with it?" he asked.

"She probably won't mind if you play with a few pieces, but I'd only do it when she's outside, just to be sure."

"Okay, good idea," he said.

Later that afternoon, when Frisky came back into the house, she wandered over to her dish for a bite of lunch.

"Hum," I heard her saying as she sniffed at the contents. "Mom must have picked up a new flavor." She took a big bite. "Interesting. I can't quite figure out what that seasoning is." She began woofing down the entire contents of the bowl.

I went into the other room and threw up.

Amanda and Andrew chose that moment to enter the kitchen. As I walked back in, I could see Andrew run toward the kitten.

"Hi Wev, I'm Andrew, and we ah gonna have so much fun!"

Rev surprised me. A lot of cats are afraid of little kids, especially if they run right up to them. But Rev just sat there, waiting patiently for Andrew to pet him. The minute Andrew's hand touched his back, that huge purring sound started.

"Wow, you weally like petting!" Andrew said as he continued to stroke Rev's back. I started to feel a little jealous. After all, this was my family, and I was sitting right there, but no one was petting me….

Amanda reached over and rubbed my ears. "It's so nice of you to take care of the kitten, Charlie," she whispered to me.

Okay, I can be a good sport. I could share my family for a few days, as long as Amanda still loved me best.

When Andrew stopped petting him, Rev made a small noise. "Meh."

I stopped rubbing against Amanda's hand. "What was that?" I asked him.

"I meowed to tell Andrew not to stop," Rev answered.

"That wasn't a meow. Try it again."

"Meh," came out in a tiny little squeak.

"That's your meow?"

He looked upset. "Yeah. Is there something wrong with it?"

"Um, er, of course not," I tried to reassure him. "It's just… unique."

"Is unique good?"

"Well, it's always good to be yourself, no matter what anyone else thinks." Was that okay? I didn't want to hurt his feelings, but that sound he made was pretty pathetic.

19

"All right." Whew.

"I'm starting to feel a little tired," Rev said when Andrew left the room. He jumped up on the couch, flopped down and fell dead asleep. Not an ear twitched, not a whisker moved. Just splat; out like a light.

I sat down on the sofa next to him and curled into a ball. After all, napping is always a great way to spend the afternoon. At least it is if you're a cat.

I woke up a while later when I heard the back door open and Frisky walked in. The family had kept Rev out of the room when she had come in to eat; I think they didn't want to overwhelm him with too much too fast. But now Frisky approached the couch, sniffing the air to see what this new visitor smelled like.

Rev woke up, jumped three feet into the air, and landed on the ground with his back arched so high that he looked like a fluffy bridge. His fur was standing straight out in every direction, plus his mouth was wide open in a silent hiss.

Frisky looked at me. "What's wrong with your friend? He looks like a hairball somebody coughed up."

"HISSSSSSS!" Rev mouthed again.

"He's never met a dog before," I said quietly

to Frisky. I walked up to Rev. "It's okay, she won't hurt you," I spoke calmly into his ear.

Apparently, he had been so focused on Frisky that he hadn't realized I had come up behind him. When he heard my voice, it startled him so much that he jumped up into the air again and landed facing me, with his eyes wide and that same hissing sound coming through his lips. "Hey!" I said sternly, "None of that. I understand you're upset, but you are a guest here and you need to use some manners!"

This was not what he was expecting. It took him so much by surprise that his eyes came back into focus and he stood just staring into my face. "It's alright," I said, "Frisky just wanted to say hello. I told you she likes cats, remember?"

He looked quickly over his shoulder at Frisky, and then back at me. "Are you sure?"

"Positive." I turned to Frisky. "Frisky, this is Rev. He'll be staying with us for a few days. Rev, this is Frisky."

"Hi!" Frisky said in her airheaded kind of way.

"Hi," Rev squeaked.

Silence. Neither of them knew how to deal with the other, so I decided to make it easier. "Frisky is in charge of security around here," I started. Frisky loves it when I make her sound like a great protector, instead of just a guard dog. "She makes sure that the family is aware of any suspicious activity in the neighborhood."

"How does she do that?" Rev asked in an awed whisper. I wasn't sure whether he was impressed or still just afraid, but at least he was talking.

"If anyone comes around the yard, or makes funny noises, or does anything strange, I bark really loud," Frisky answered.

"Really?" Rev turned to me and whispered, "What does that mean?"

"Barking is a deep sound that dogs make to alert people to trouble," I replied.

"I'll show you," Frisky said, and she began opening her mouth.

"No, Frisky don't…" I cried.

Too late. Frisky let out a huge, deep, growly bark.

Rev jumped so high I thought his head was going to hit the ceiling. His eyes were wider than I remembered his face being, and his orange fur made him three times his normal size. He didn't even seem to hit the ground, but landed at a dead run, heading straight into the bedroom and under Andrew's bed faster than you could blink.

"Oops, sorry," Frisky gulped.

"I'll take care of it," I answered, as I walked slowly back to the bedroom.

I found him cowering in a little ball. "Are you okay? Frisky's really sorry. She didn't mean to scare you."

"Oh, I wasn't scared," Rev replied as he came out from under the bed shaking violently. "I just figured that I hadn't seen this room yet, so I wanted to check it out." He looked around like he was casually exploring. "Yeah, nothing too exciting under there," he said as he looked back under the bed.

Yeah, right. Oh well, no use embarrassing him any more than he had already embarrassed himself.

23

"This is Andrew's room."

"Oh, the kid who was petting me before? He seems real nice."

"Everybody here is nice, including Frisky, and even Rose."

"Who's Rose?"

Just as Rev asked this question, a big yellow ball came rolling up behind us. Now, I am quite used to seeing Rose in her hamster ball. Actually, I can't see her, because my eyes can't see through that funny color of plastic, but I know she's in there and that she can make the ball move. I was about to explain this when Rev went running up to it.

"Wow! What a huge, awesome ball!" He hit it with his paw and sent it rolling the other direction. "Sweet!" he yelled as he batted the ball again and chased after it.

"Whoa! Stop it!" I heard Rose scream from inside the ball.

"How cool! It's a talking ball! Watch me jump on it, Charlie!"

"Rev, stop!" I shouted.

"Cut it out!" Rose was screeching.

But Rev wasn't listening. He jumped up on top of the big ball. He was small enough that he could actually land all four paws up there and balance around.

"Wow, it has a really neat smell, too. This house has the best toys!"

I ran across the room and stood right in front of the ball. "Rev, get down from there, now!"

He looked at me very sadly and stepped down to the floor. "What's the matter, Charlie? Are you mad at me? I thought you were my friend. Am I not allowed to play with your ball?"

As he looked at me, those big eyes started to fill up with tears. He looked so forlorn that I almost told him to jump back up there again. Then I remembered Rose.

"No, you don't understand. I'm not mad at you. There's another animal inside that ball. You're going to hurt her if you play with it while she's in there."

"There's a creature in there? That's what smells so good." In a quick change of emotion, Rev went from looking sad to looking wild. "Is it a mouse? Or a rat? Or some other tasty morsel?" His mouth began to water.

"Her name is Rose, and she's a hamster." He looked like he was about to pounce on the ball. I put my paw on his shoulder to hold him still. "You are not allowed to eat her. She's a member of this family, just like the rest of us. She is actually very smart and you would be wise to make friends with her. That is, if

25

she'll speak to you after this." I walked over to the ball. "Rose, are you okay in there?"

"Oh, my aching head!" I heard a little voice say. "Charlie, what was that? All I saw was orange fur and paws and... it was a cat, wasn't it?"

"Yeah, sorry about that Rose. This is Rev," I signaled for him to come over and stand next to me. "He's just a kitten, so he didn't know any better." Rev just stood there, staring at the ball, trying to see through the plastic.

"Humph. I liked you're first reaction to seeing me in my sphere a lot better than his." When I had seen Rose rolling in that thing the first time, I had thought that the ball was alive and trying to get me. I ran around the whole house while she chased me. Since I was trying to convince Rev that I was brave, I didn't really want him hearing that story.

"Well," I interrupted quickly, "If you're okay now, we'll leave you alone. Maybe we'll come back later and visit when you're in your cage and Rev can see you."

"Fine. But if he ever tries anything like that again, I'll, I'll, I'll...."

I almost laughed. Even though Rev was just a kitten, he was still five times the size of a hamster. "I know Rose. You'll find some way to make him sorry."

"That's right. You see if I don't." With that, she rolled herself away.

"Wow. She's kind of bossy, huh? You sure I can't just eat her?" Rev asked.

"Positive. She's part of the family. Just stay out of her way and you'll be fine."

"Okay," he said in a disappointed tone. Then he looked up toward the living room. "What's that?" he shouted as he dashed away to chase a fly buzzing past.

Kittens.

Chapter 3

A Cry in the Night

THE SOUND of crying woke me up in the middle of the night.

It had been easy to convince Rev to sleep on Amanda's bed with me. When he had started to look a little tired, I told him to come with me to say goodnight to her. I came in every night at bedtime; I would snuggle up next to Amanda as she settled into bed each night, and she would pet me gently until she fell asleep. Rev and I had jumped up onto the bed (Rev had to make the jump three times before he got high enough to actually land on top), and both of us had curled up next to my favorite girl. Amanda only had to stroke Rev twice and he fell fast asleep. She had smiled at me about that, and then continued to pet me until we were both asleep.

The tears that disturbed my dreams were very

quiet. I opened my eyes and saw Rev, stilled curled up next to me, sniffing and wiping his eyes.

"Are you okay?" I asked sleepily.

He tried for a minute to straighten himself up and pretend he hadn't been crying. I could see him taking deep breaths and trying to gulp down the big lump in his throat. It didn't work. He let out a little wail, "I miss Jeffery!"

"Who's Jeffery?" I asked.

"My little boy. I sleep with him every night. I like to crawl up on the pillow, right next to his head, and snuggle into his hair to sleep. That way, if I wake up in the middle of the night, it feels just like laying against my mom's fur." He took a deep breath and sniffed again. "I don't know why I'm here. Why did they send me away? Doesn't Jeffery love me anymore? Am I a bad kitten, and they just don't want me?"

He looked so sad that I almost wanted to cry with him. "No, it's not like that," I told him. "I heard the lady when she dropped you off. She said it was only for a few days." I paused for a moment, trying to think. "Maybe they had to go on a trip, or someone was coming to visit that was allergic to cats," I offered.

"I don't think so," Rev said slowly. "Jeffery was coughing and wheezing and not sleeping very well the last few nights. I don't think they would have taken him on vacation right now." He paused for a moment. "I'm really worried about him," Rev whispered. "I think maybe he was getting very sick, and now I'm not there to take care of him and make him feel better. He always says that being with me makes him happy. I'm afraid he's going to be sick and sad both at the same time."

Suddenly, this pain-in-the-neck little creature didn't seem so irritating. He was very important to somebody. I tried to imagine how I would feel if Mom dropped me off somewhere without telling me why, and I thought that something might be wrong with Amanda. I reached over and rubbed my head against her leg to reassure myself that she was okay.

"Don't worry yourself over something you're not sure about," I heard myself saying. "You don't know if Jeffery is sick or not. Maybe he got better and is out someplace having fun. Try to think about that tonight so you can get some sleep. Tomorrow, I'll help you figure out what's really going on. If Jeffery needs you, we'll find a way to get you to him."

"Really?" He looked up at me with a smile. "Charlie, you're the nicest, bravest, most wonderful cat I ever met."

I felt myself getting all warm inside. "Come here," I said to him. He laid down next to me, and I put my paw around him. "Just get some sleep, and we'll find out the details in the morning."

I could feel the tension leave his body. He fell back to sleep within moments. I smiled, thinking that I had found the right words to make him feel better.

I had no idea to what I had just committed myself.

Chapter 4

Telephone and Tag

PROMISING TO do something is easy; doing it is something else. When I opened my eyes in the morning, Rev was already awake. He was sitting very quietly, just staring at my face with those big, brown eyes. "What are you looking at?" I asked sleepily.

"You are so awesome," he said in a hushed voice. "I don't know how you're gonna do it, but I just know you'll get me back to Jeffery."

Oh, yeah. I had kind of forgotten about that while I was sleeping, and in truth, I was hoping he would forget it too. I had no idea how I was going to find out what was going on, let alone, fix it.

But, as I looked into that face, seeing him look at me like I was some kind of hero, I knew I had to try. No, not try. I had to do it.

I thought about the problem while Rev and I ate breakfast. I considered going over to Rev's house to see if anyone was home. If the house stayed empty all day, then I could tell him his family was definitely on a trip, and that they would come to get him when they returned. I could also look in the window and make sure the furniture was still there. I couldn't imagine someone moving and leaving a sweet little kitten behind, but you never know.

There was a problem with that plan, because I had no idea where Rev lived. He had been in a box while traveling in the car, so there was no way he could tell me which direction to go or how far away it was.

Scratch that idea.

I considered my outside sources of information. The cats around here keep close track of everything that goes on, and dogs are always nosy neighbors, so I can usually find out anything I want to know by just checking with the animals that live nearby. However, I didn't think any of my friends could help this time. Unless Rev lived within two blocks of my house, none of the neighborhood animals would have any info.

Another idea down the drain.

Just as I was beginning to lose hope, the telephone rang. That was it! Whenever I get really bored, I listen to Mom or Amanda talk on the phone. I can

33

usually pick up all kinds of interesting information about people and places just by hearing one end of the conversation. Sometimes it gets a little aggravating, when they say things like, "She did! No, tell me she didn't do that!" and I have no idea who "she" is or what "that" was, but if I listen long enough, I can usually figure it out. Rev obviously came from a family who loved him. I was pretty sure they would be calling to check on him sometime in the next couple of days. If I eavesdropped on every phone call, I would be able to figure out what was happening and when they would be coming back to get him.

Unfortunately, the phone didn't ring the rest of the morning. Rev must have chased every piece of dog food from Frisky's bowl, each speck of dust in the house and every single fly that existed, as I sat patiently waiting for the phone to ring. In a way, it was nice to have an excuse not to run after him the whole morning, because this kid had way too much energy, and I didn't think I'd be able to keep up. Yet, some of what he was doing looked fun, and I would have enjoyed playing with him.

Eventually I realized that I could hear the phone ring from anywhere in the house, so when I saw Rev toss Catnip in the air (Catnip is my toy mouse), I ran over and snatched it before it hit the ground. He looked upset at first, but then I smiled at him, and he realized I was just playing. I took off running across the room with Rev chasing behind me. He may have been fast and full of energy, but I had longer legs and could leap a lot farther than any kitten. I also knew the house better than he did, so I could race around corners knowing what was coming. Rev, on the other hand, actually hit the wall twice running around the turns too quickly.

I stopped long enough to make sure he was okay and then kept going.

I was just starting to tire out when I heard the phone ringing. "Here, take this," I said, as I tossed Catnip over to Rev and ran to the kitchen. I got there just as Mom was saying, "Hello."

"Oh, hi. I'm so glad you called. How's Jeffery doing?" I heard her say. "Uh, huh... Oh, that's too bad... Poor thing... How long do they think they'll have to keep him there?... Which hospital?... Saint Joseph's?... Well, let him know we're taking good care of Rev, maybe that will help him feel better... Yeah, he and Charlie seem to be having a great time together... I understand. No problem. You just let me know if there's anything else we can do to help. You try to get some rest too, all right? Take care, and we'll be praying for Jeffery...Goodbye." Mom hung up with a sigh.

Hospital? Poor thing? This was not good. Something was horribly wrong with Jeffery if he had to stay at the hospital.

I looked over at Mom. She looked really worried. How was I going to tell Rev that something bad was happening to his special boy?

Chapter 5

We've Got Trouble

WHAT WAS I supposed to do? Rev was just a baby, I didn't think he would be able to fully understand or deal with having his special boy in trouble.

I paced around the living room for quite a while, trying to figure out what to do and what to say. Finally, I realized there was no easy way to do this. I couldn't just say, "By the way, Jeffery is sick, but come on, let's play!" I would have to tell him straight out and then help him to handle it.

I found him in Mom's bedroom trying to open the closet door. "I can smell something really good in there," he said when he saw me. "It's not a dead animal, but it kinda smells like one."

"It's shoes," I said, rolling my eyes.

"Un-uh. I've smelled shoes. They're like

plasticy or cloth. This is different."

"They're leather shoes," I explained.

"What's leather?"

"I think it's made from a cow."

"There's a cow in there?" he screamed in excitement.

"No," I smiled, "just a cows skin."

"They took its skin off? Eww, it must look really disgusting walking around with no skin on!"

I didn't explain. "Rev, we need to have a talk."

He got serious very quickly. "You found out something about Jeffery, didn't you?" he asked quietly.

"Yes." I took a deep breath while he sat down on the floor next to me. He looked up with his eyes full of hope. "Do you know what a hospital is?" I asked.

"No. Is it somewhere you go on vacation?"

"No. It's a place people go when they are very sick. It's like the vet, but for people, and they have to stay there until they get well."

"Why are you telling me this?" he whispered fearfully.

"Because Jeffery is in the hospital. I don't know what's wrong with him, but he must be in bad shape if they are keeping him there."

I reached over and set one of my paws on top of one of his. I was ready for the tears. I was ready for him to cry and moan and go crazy with worry.

"I have to get to him," Rev said very calmly.

Huh? It took me a moment to change gears. He looked so calm and determined when I had expected hysterics. "Rev, you can't go to the hospital. It's for people. Besides, there's nothing you could do there. Jeffery will be home as soon as the people vet makes him better."

"You don't understand," he spoke very firmly. "Jeffery has been sick before. Not so bad he had to be taken away for a long time, but still sick. Sometimes he has a hard time breathing," he explained. "It scared me the first time it happened. Jeffery was lying on his bed, his mom was sitting next to him, and he was so white and his chest was going up and down, and he was making all this noise when he tried to breath. I didn't know what to do. Then I remembered that when I was really little, and I didn't feel good or I was afraid, my mom would cuddle up next to me. It would make me feel better. So I jumped up on the bed next to Jeffery, and I rubbed my head against his hand. I just wanted him to know I was there and that I loved him. But pretty soon, he started petting my cheeks with his hand, and his breathing seemed to get a little easier. The longer I stayed there, letting him pet me and loving on him, the better he got.

"From then on, every time Jeffery felt bad, I would jump up on the bed and rub against him. I helped him to feel better. If he's sick now, then he needs me more than ever. I'm going to him, no matter what it takes," he said in a very strong voice.

Wow. I just sat there for a moment, looking at this amazing kitten. I thought he was going to fall apart when he heard the news, but instead, he took it in stride and was ready to help.

Unfortunately, it was time for a reality check. "Rev, I think it's great that you want to help your boy. He's going to remember the fact that you've been there for him before, and it will help him to be strong. But you can't go to the hospital."

"Why not?"

"Well, for one thing, we don't know where the hospital is. We don't know how to get there, and it's a big world outside. Trust me, I've seen it, and it can be very scary. Even if we found out where it was and we made it there, animals aren't allowed. I've seen it on TV. They wouldn't let us in the door, let alone into Jeffery's room."

For a moment he wavered. He hadn't realized

how many problems could stand in the way. Then he got an excited look in his eyes. "You said we!"

"What?"

"You said if we got there. That means you're willing to help me find it!" He just looked at me and smiled. "Charlie, you are the smartest, bravest, most amazing cat I have ever met. I know you're going to find a way to get me to Jeffery."

"I really don't see how," I told him.

"It doesn't matter. I just know you're going to figure it out." His voice took on a pleading tone. "I have to go to him, Charlie. I have to be there for him. What would you do if it were Amanda?"

I didn't say anything for a moment or two. I just sat there, wondering what it would feel like if anyone in my family were in trouble, and what I would do if I thought I could help them. "Okay, I'll see what I can figure out." He looked like he was about to do a happy dance, so I added quickly, "I can't promise anything. I have no clue how to do this, but I'll really try."

He jumped up and rubbed his cheek against mine. "Thank you, Charlie! I know whatever plan you come up with, it's going to work!"

I wished that I could share his enthusiasm.

Chapter 6

Flying Cats?

WHEN YOU don't have the answer to a question, the first thing you need to do is ask someone who might know. All I had to do was figure out who could tell me where the hospital was and how to get there. Then I would just come up with a plan to sneak Rev and myself out of the house, through the town, into the hospital, and up to Jeffery's room. That's all.

Yeah, right.

Mom was the only one that I was sure would know where the hospital was located. Unfortunately, there was no way I could communicate my question to her. Believe me, I tried. But no amount of rubbing against her or meowing at her or pawing at her arm would get me directions. I figured Dad probably knew the way, but the same problem existed.

Maybe some animal in the neighborhood would know! I asked Frisky, but if she had ever known, the answer had long since left her head along with every other piece of input. Since I was in the back yard, I jumped up on the fence to ask Pepe.

Pepe is the Chihuahua next door. When I looked over into his yard, he was standing at the back door of his house jumping up and down. I mean, he was jumping straight up into the air about two feet, landing, and then leaping up again.

I watched him for a couple of minutes and then called over. "Hey Pepe, I need to talk to you."

"Not now, man. It's walk time!" As he jumped up and down, he started yapping over and over, "Walk, walk, walk!"

"You're as bad as the kitten," I said without thinking.

He stopped jumping. He turned and looked at me with a really angry glint in his eyes. "Did choo jus' say I look like a cat?"

"No, that's not what I meant," I started to apologize. Pepe is a very small dog with big ears, so I knew he was sensitive about his looks.

But he interrupted me. "I am a champion Chihuahua. I have a room full of ribbons and trophies that say I am the best dog around. My Frank," he motioned toward the back door with his head, so I would know he was talking about his special person inside, "he has offers from dogs all over the country, man, wanting me to be the father of their puppies. I don't want any of them, because I only want my little love Frisky, but the point is the same, I am *The Dog*, man. I am the best."

Wow. That was really kind of sweet, and slightly disturbing.

I tried again. "I'm sorry if I offended you Pepe, but I wasn't saying you look like a kitten. I just meant the way that you were jumping up and down reminded me of the kitten who is visiting with us right now."

"Oh. Okay then," he calmed right down. "Well, it looks like Frank is running slow for my walk man, so what choo need?"

"Do you know where the hospital is?" I asked.

"Hmm, no. I heard of the hospital before, but I never been there. Why choo want to know?"

I explained the situation with Rev. "Can you think of anyone who would know where it is?" I asked when I had finished.

"Not right away, but I'll think about it. I don't know if it will help though. I mean, what's this kitten think he's gonna do? He's not like magic or somethin,' is he?"

"No."

"'Cause that would be really cool man. Can choo imagine? A magic cat. It's like he would wave his tail over this Jeffery dude, and then he would jus' sit up and be better," he paused for a moment. "And maybe he could fly too, choo know? Maybe he would have hidden wings, and jus' pull them out and fly up into the sky to save all the little kitties everywhere." He was looking very excited.

I just stared at him for a minute. "Yeah, that would be really cool, Pepe, but he's not a magic cat. He's just a regular kitten who wants to help his special boy."

"Okay, well, I'll check with some of the other dogs around here and see if anybody knows where the hospital is, man. It would be a lot easier to find it and get there if he could fly though."

"Yeah, it would, but we have to deal with reality here."

"Too bad." Then the back door of his house started to open, and he went sailing up into the air again. "Walk, walk walk!" he shouted and ran inside.

Okay.

Well, since Pepe was going to be asking the dogs in the neighborhood, maybe I should check with all the cats. The best way to do that was to hit the Kit-Cat Club.

Chapter 7

The Elvis Impersonator

THE KIT-KAT is a blues club that's just for cats. It's right down the block from my house in someone's back yard and hidden behind a hedge. All the felines in the area hang out there to hear some good blues music and just kick back with their friends. It's a great place.

I went into the house to have some dinner and wait until the sun went down. That's when all my friends would be heading to the club.

Rev was chasing a piece of dog food when I walked into the kitchen. He quickly put it into Andrew's shoe and came running over to me. "Any ideas yet, Charlie?"

"Not yet, but I'm working on it," I assured

him.

"What are we gonna' do now?" he asked.

"I don't know about you, but I'm going to get some food and take a quick nap. I'm going out tonight to see if I can get some information that will help us."

"Great! I'll go too," he said, as he began chasing his tail.

"No. You can get some food with me, and you can take a nap with me, but you're not going out with me tonight."

"How come?" his little face dropped.

Because you'll drive me crazy, I thought to myself. But, out loud I said, "This is grown-up stuff. The cats I'm going to talk to are all adults, and they might not like it if I brought a kitten to the club with me."

"The club? What club? What's it called? Where is it? Do you have to be a member? Do they wear funny hats? Do they have a secret pawshake?"

I just ignored his questions, walked over and started eating. He kept talking, even as he was stuffing food into his mouth. He continued asking silly questions about where I was going after we finished eating and went over to the couch. He kept asking as we lay there. In fact, he actually fell asleep halfway through a question.

About an hour later, I woke up and quietly slipped down off the sofa and over to the back door. Rev was sound asleep, and I wanted him to stay that way. I needed to concentrate on figuring out how to help him, and all his questions were not only making that harder, but they were driving me nuts!

Mom let me out the door with a warning to be back before it got too late, and I set off down the street.

When I arrived at the entrance to the club, I could already hear music playing and someone singing. I walked in and looked around, hoping to spot my friend Blackie. Blackie was the very first cat I met when we moved to Arizona, and he's a great guy. I saw him sitting at a make-shift table near the back, so I went right up to him.

"Charlie, my friend, how are you!" He greeted me in his deep, raspy voice. He grinned and reached out a paw for a high five.

"I'm doing great, but I have a little problem." I told him about Rev, his situation, and the help that I needed.

"Well, I don't know where the hospital is. My person has been there a few times, but they always take him away in a loud, screaming van when he needs to go. It makes a horrible sound, so I always hide in the back of the house until they leave. I don't even know which direction it is." He looked thoughtful for a moment. "You need to get your problem out for everyone to hear at once Charlie, and you know there's only one way to do that."

"You want me to sing a song on stage, don't you?" I asked.

"Yeah, that's right. But you got another problem. It's Elvis night tonight, so you can only sing his tunes."

Elvis Presley. The King of "Rock and Roll." Well, he had lots of songs, so it should be easy to choose one. I just had to figure out which one....

"Okay, Blackie. Can you get the band to play 'Heartbreak Hotel' for me?"

He smiled. "Oh, yeah. I'll even sit in on the

saxophone."

When the pretty girl cat that was onstage finished her song, Blackie walked up and talked to the band. Then he signaled for me to come on up there.

I always get nervous when I sing on stage, so I was shaking a little when I started. I just kept reminding myself how important this was, and tried to forget my nerves as I sang:

I'm trying to help this kitten,
Rev is his name.
He's really a nice kid,
But, he's a little bit insane.

This little kitten,
This silly kitten,
Will drive me crazy by and by.

He eats my cat food, I mean
He scarfs it by the pound.
And when he tries to talk
He makes a squeaky little sound.

This little kitten, my friends
This silly kitten
Will drive me crazy by and by.

His family has a problem
His boy is really ill
So I need to help him find the way
To the hos-pi-till

Please can you help me? My friend,
Please can you help me,
To get this kitten to his boy?

When I stopped singing the whole club was quiet for a minute. I thought maybe they were all mad at me for changing the words, but then they started clapping. As I walked back to Blackie's table, several cats stopped me to talk. Many of them had stories to tell of irritating kittens that they had met, or about family members going to the hospital, but none of them seemed to know how to get there.

I stayed around for several hours, talking to as many cats as I could, but no one knew where the hospital was.

I went home feeling a little frantic. I hoped Rev would be sleeping, since I still hadn't worked out a plan to help him.

Chapter 8

All the News Worth Barking

WE FINALLY got a break the next morning. I was in the backyard with Andrew, who was picking dandelions and blowing the fuzzy white seeds off the top. He was aiming them toward the back door, where Rev was standing inside the house, and Rev was trying to catch the little puffy things by reaching his paws under the screen.

"Charlie, look!" he yelled after a few minutes. "I caught a fairy! That means my wish will come true! And you know what I wish for, right?"

"To help Jeffery?"

"Yep. This means your gonna find the answer today!" He squealed as Andrew blew another flower, and the seeds scattered in the wind again.

It was good that he thought so, because I was beginning to give up hope. I had no clue as to how or who to ask for information. I was stumped.

"Hey, Charlie!" I heard Pepe call from next door. "Jump up here and talk to me. I think I got some help for choo."

I leaped the six feet to land on top of the fence. "What's up?" I asked.

"I'm getting some info through the neighborhood dog chain. Hold on a sec," he turned away from me and barked over the next fence.

The neighborhood dog chain is how dogs get the news and gossip from all over. If any dog has news to tell, he barks it to the closest dogs on either side of him, and they pass it to the next dogs, and so on and so on. At times the news can travel for hundreds of miles, if the dogs think it's interesting enough. Sometimes it's about burglars and other important information. Occasionally it's about a cute little poodle that moved in two blocks away. Usually, it is the latest rabbit hunting report from those dogs that love to chase and want to share their latest "It escaped down the hole again," story with everyone.

Most of it is a lot of nonsense, and I usually ignore it when Frisky tries to tell me what she has heard. After all, if it's anything important, I'll hear it from my cat friends. Most dog news, well, it's just so… canine.

So, as Pepe barked his little head off, I just waited calmly, with the hope that he wasn't about to tell me how Rover down the street buried another bone and now can't find it.

"H'okay, I think we may have found a way for

choo to get the kitten to the hospi… hospi… choo know, the medicine place," he finally choked out.

"How?" I asked in excitement.

"Well, choo know Stripe, the spotty Dalmatian down the street? Well, he says his owner is eating chips and sausage while watching the football games today."

"So?" I was trying to be patient, but what did this have to do with anything?

"So, this dude has a problem, man. Every time he eats like that and sits around watching TV, he gets bad heartburn. When he complains about it, his wife thinks he's havin' a heart attack, and she calls the ambulance. He's really okay, and he gets mad because he always has to miss the end of the game, while talking to the paramedics, but choo know how wives can be."

Not having a wife, I really didn't know, but that was not the issue right now. "Okay, an ambulance is coming. How does that help us?"

"Choo really runnin' a little slow in the brain today, huh Charlie? When they're done checkin' the guy, they'll go back to the hospital. Choo can follow them all the way there."

"I may be running a little slow in the brain, but my feet aren't nearly fast enough to keep up with a car! Any bright ideas on how I'm supposed to do that, especially since I'll have a baby kitten with me? His legs are shorter than yours!"

"My legs are not short!" he shouted back at me. "They are jus' perfect for my macho "show-dog" body. Anyway, I can't think of everything."

"Whatever. How do I know when the ambulance is coming?"

"Jus' listen for the sirens, man. When they come, they always blast those loud things."

"Thanks for the help, Pepe. I'll see what I can figure out from here." I jumped back down into our yard.

It was time for a serious plan. As soon as we heard the sirens, I had to get Rev out of the house, into the front yard, and running as fast as a moving car. Yeah, right.

Then it hit me. I knew what I had to do. It wouldn't be easy, and it would require some outside help, but it could work. It had to.

Chapter 9

To the Rescue!

For my of plan to work, Rev and I would have to be in the front yard when the ambulance arrived. Since he was only visiting, Mom hadn't let the kitten out of the house. That way, he couldn't get lost or try to run away. I would have to sneak him out, and it would have to be through the front door, since he was too little to jump the back fence.

Frisky and human nature were the perfect answers. I asked Frisky to come into the house and explained what I needed. She agreed right away. The fact that it was something she loved to do anyway helped a lot. Then I went to get Rev ready.

"Okay Rev, this is going to take stealth, perfect timing, and a little luck. When we hear the sirens, you have to be ready to do everything as planned, no looking back. So, if you're having any second thoughts, tell me now, before it's too late."

"No way, Charlie. I'm going to go help Jeffery, no matter what it takes."

"Just stay focused. It's like in action movies; everything depends on you doing exactly what I say, or our mission will fail."

He smiled. "I feel like some kind of super spy," he giggled.

So, as we hid behind the big chair near the front door, waiting for our adventure to begin, the theme song from 'Mission Impossible' kept running through my head. That's just what I needed to make this whole thing complete: background music.

Instead, we had the sound of a football game. Dad was watching his favorite team play in the front room. It must have been a good game, since he kept jumping up and yelling at the TV. Each time he leapt into the air, either yelling, "YES!" or "GO!" or "Nooo...!!" Rev would jump to attention.

"Is that the siren?" he would ask in excitement.

This went on for a long time. At the beginning of the game, Rev and I had both stood waiting behind the chair, our legs tense and our ears straining to hear any sound that might mean it was time to spring into action. After two hours, Rev was asleep at my feet, and I sat listening to the game, wondering if I had time for a nap, too. Just as I was starting to lie down, we heard a loud noise coming from far away.

"What's that?" Rev asked, leaping to his feet.

"I think," I strained my ears to hear better, "I think that's the ambulance!"

Now, Frisky may not be the sharpest crayon in the box, but she has great ears. She had been lying at Dad's feet, begging for potato chips and waiting for the real action to begin. Before I heard a sound, she was already up and putting our plan into action. She nudged Dad's leg and then ran to the refrigerator and looked up. That's where her leash was stored, and this was her signal to Dad that she wanted to take a walk.

"Not now, Frisky. It's the middle of the game," Dad told her. But just then, he heard the wailing of sirens.

If there's one thing I understand, it's curiosity (you know the old expression about what it can do to a cat). People are very similar to cats in that way; they like to know what's going on, especially if it's something new and different. So I was counting on the fact that Dad would want to know what the sirens were all about.

"Okay Frisky," he said while walking over to get the leash. "We'll go see what's going on. But, it's probably just George getting indigestion again."

As he hooked the leash onto Frisky's collar, I whispered to Rev. "Okay, get ready."

Frisky led Dad to the door, excitement showing in her every step. The very way she moved reminded me of Pepe, seeming to scream, "Walk, walk, walk!"

As soon as Dad opened the door, Frisky turned to look at me, winked, and then ran in a circle around Dad. As Dad struggled to turn around after her, trying to get untangled from the leash, Rev and I dashed out the open door.

"Quick, in here!" I shouted as we cleared the porch and jumped into a big bush. Right behind us, but unaware that we had just escaped, Dad walked out and closed the door.

We stayed hidden in the shrub as Dad and Frisky headed down the street. "Okay, we have to stay back from them, until Frisky pulls Dad in another direction, so he doesn't spot us" I told Rev.

"Okay," he answered behind me, but his voice sounded a little strange. I turned to look at him and found him staring all around. "Wow, the world is really big," he said in an awed voice.

"You've never been outside before?"

"No," he answered. "It's so big," he repeated.

Uh-oh. This was something I had not anticipated. When you live inside, you get used to having a ceiling over your head and walls all around you that define the size of your world. When you step outside for the first time, you tend to get overwhelmed by the unending vastness of it all.

We did not have time for Rev to be overwhelmed.

"Rev, I need you to look at me for a minute," I pushed his face with my paw until he was staring right into my eyes. "I know that this is kind of big, scary, and exciting all at the same time. If we could, I'd let you just stand here and stare and explore to your heart's content, but we have an assignment to accomplish. We have to get to that ambulance before it leaves, and we only have a little time to do it. Once this is over, after you've gotten to see Jeffery and know that everything is okay, then I promise we'll find the time to let you go wild and play outside. But for now, you have to concentrate. Understand?"

That determined look came back into his eyes. "Got it Boss."

Boss. I liked that. "Stay right behind me," I told him.

I snuck from bush to bush, with Rev right on my tail. We made our way from our yard, to the one next-door, and then slowly down the street until we were directly across the sidewalk from where the ambulance was parked. The back doors were open, so I leapt over the cement and onto the back bumper.

I stared into the back of the vehicle as Rev landed beside me. It was kind of scary; it was like a big van, but instead of regular seats, there was all this equipment. On one side, a bottle of liquid was hanging from the wall, with all kinds of tubes coming out of the bottom. There were shelves on the walls, with different kinds of medical stuff all closed in behind clear doors. Strapped on the floor was a big metal tank that was labeled "Oxygen," and there was a tube coming off it that was attached to a mask. On the opposite side, there was a bench with seats on it. I guessed that's where the paramedics would sit while they worked on the patient. The middle was empty, so I figured that was where the hurt person would lie on the way to the hospital. Getting my bearings, I noticed that the bench had a big storage space underneath. Perfect. I signaled to Rev, and we crawled beneath the seats.

It was crowded inside; there were big toolbox like things and other stuff all shoved in, so that no matter what kind of trouble a person was in, these people would be able to get to them and help. Luckily, Rev was still small, because I don't think both of us would have fit otherwise. We went a long way in; it was like a very small tunnel we had to make our way through, but I didn't want to be spotted by anyone when the paramedics came back.

As we hid under there, we could hear the radio in the front of the ambulance. I guess a lot of people must get sick and hurt, because there was all kinds of noise from other ambulances and someone called "Dispatch," talking to each other and to the hospital.

"Charlie," Rev whispered to me, "It's scary in here."

"Yeah, I know," I shivered. "Just hang on. Hopefully we won't have to stay here very long."

"Can I just climb out for a few minutes?" he started backing slowly out of the cubby while he spoke. "It's just so small. I feel like I can hardly breath...."

"No Rev, you really shouldn't..." I was trying to get him to stay where he was, so no one would spot us, but I didn't need to bother. Just as he started to move, we heard a loud noise near the back door, and Rev ducked behind me again.

"Well, that didn't take as long as it usually does," said a deep voice. We could hear a funny noise, and I realized they were rolling a flat bed into the ambulance. There was no one on it.

"Yeah. I think his wife is finally starting to believe us when we tell her it's just heartburn," said another voice.

"It won't be for much longer if that guy keeps eating all that fatty food," the first voice laughed. He said something else, but I couldn't hear him. A huge red toolbox was being shoved into the storage area where we were hiding, and I was about to get smashed! I backed up farther and then farther, until I was almost standing on top of Rev, who was already lying on top of some other rescue stuff. I opened my mouth to scream, because otherwise I was going to be squished....

And it stopped. The medics closed the back doors and walked around to the front of the ambulance. They climbed in and started the engine. Our drive was about to begin.

I must take a moment here to remind you of how much I hate riding in cars. I don't know how I get myself into these things, but somehow I always end up taking a drive somewhere, when I would prefer any other mode of travel. I could walk, run, or be carried. Hey, I might even enjoy flying, but somehow I continually end up in a car.

Worse than that, I was in a truck again. The only other time I'd ridden in the back of a truck, I got smashed by all the stuff that was in there every time the driver took a turn. Looking around the cramped space where Rev and I were, I knew there would be big trouble if anything moved.

Lucky for us, we figured out very quickly that everything inside the ambulance had a special place that was designed to keep things from flying around. That made sense, because otherwise, when they were rushing a sick or injured person to the hospital, that person would be in worse shape by the time they got there than when they had started.

So Rev and I held our positions, with Rev trying not to freak out over being in such a small space (have you ever heard of claustrophobia?), and me trying not to yowl or screech or any of the other things I naturally do when closed in the back of a car.

Finally, the vehicle came to a stop and the two

people in the front got out. Uh-oh. What if they just left and didn't come to the back? I hadn't thought about that!

Luck was still with us, because they immediately opened the back doors. I found out later that an ambulance has to be cleaned out each time it gets used.

"Okay Rev, let's see if we can get out of here," I whispered.

I started crawling forward. It was really a tight squeeze, but I could feel Rev right behind me as I worked my way around the big toolbox and out to the opening of the storage area. When I got right to the end, I stopped to make sure the coast was clear. The medics were standing there, wiping things down.

"Rev, I'm going to count to three. On three, you and I are going to run as fast as we can and get out of this thing. Are you ready?"

"Yes," he squeaked.

"Okay. One, two, three!"

I slipped out of the storage area, ran the last few steps to the back door, and leaped onto the ground. I could feel Rev right behind me.

"Was that a cat?" I heard one of the medics ask.

"No, I think it was two cats!" the other one

answered.

We didn't stick around to find out if they were upset or not about our stowing away in their van. We were in the hospital parking lot, and Jeffery was inside somewhere needing Rev.

Chapter 10

Havoc in the Hospital

WE HID behind the tires of another ambulance, so we could figure out our next move. Both vehicles were parked several feet away from a ramp leading up to two big swinging doors. People were walking in and out, and the sign overhead said "Emergency."

"Okay, Rev, get ready," I told him. "The next time a person walks up the ramp to go inside, we're going to follow him or her. We have to stay behind, so the person won't see us, but we have to be right behind, so we can get in the doors while they're open. Are you ready?"

"Ready," he said in a quivering voice.

I turned to look at him. He was shaking all over, from his whiskers to the tip of his tail. "Are you sure you're okay?" I asked him.

"Yeah, I'm just a little scared," he answered quietly. "I really want Jeffery to be okay, and I don't know what's wrong with him or how to help him for sure."

"Remember what you told me before? You said you help Jeffery just by being near him. Whatever is wrong, you being here is going to be good for him."

He smiled. "You're the best, Charlie." He took a deep breath. "I'm ready now," and his tail popped up into the air, signaling that he was prepared to run.

We didn't wait long. A man came hurrying toward the door, looking very worried, so I guessed he must have been there to see someone who was hurt or sick. As he started up the ramp, I slipped close behind him, right on his heels, making sure Rev was with me. The man opened the door, and we jumped through before it could close.

There was a lot of noise inside. I ran and hid behind a big potted plant with Rev right beside me.

We were in a waiting room. I knew that, because there was a bunch of people just sitting around waiting. There was a TV up in the corner playing the football game and lots of magazines lying around. There were all kinds of different people sitting around the room, some of them hurt, others giving comfort. I guessed this must be where they had to stay until

71

the doctor could see them. We could hear people in the exam rooms beyond, some of them crying, and it was really kind of scary....

"What next Charlie?" I heard Rev ask.

Snap out of it Charlie, I told myself. You have work to do.

"This is probably where they brought Jeffery when he first got to the hospital," I told him.

"No problem then, I'll just sniff around until I pick up his scent. Then we'll follow it to where ever he is now!" Rev stated. He started smelling everything, but it didn't take him long to give up that idea. "Everything smells like disinfectant!" he said as he scrunched up his nose.

"Let's just watch for a few minutes, and see where people go from here," I told him.

The first thing I figured out about hospitals is that nurses are very nice people. Everyone in that room was either hurt or worried about someone that was injured, but the nice ladies and men who worked there tried really hard to calm them all down and make them comfortable. After a little while, one of the women came out of the back pushing a man in a wheel chair.

"All right now, Mr. Barr, the doctor says you're going to be spending the night here, so I'm going to take you to a room."

"Okay Rev, follow that nurse!" I whispered.

We sneaked behind her hoping no one would notice us. Luckily, everyone in the hospital was very busy, so no one seemed to look down. We followed them through a long hallway, turned, and went down another hallway past a big metal door. I stopped at the door and pulled Rev to the side. The nurse and her patient kept going.

"Why are we stopping Charlie?"

I didn't answer right away. The door had a list next to it showing all the different kinds of patients that might be in the hospital. It said things like, Emergency, ICU, Labor and Delivery, and a bunch of other things that I didn't understand. But what stood out from all the rest, were the words, CHILDREN'S WARD. Each of the areas had a number next to it. "I'm not sure, but I think that door might take us to Jeffery," I told Rev.

"Okay, I'll get it open!" he said and started shoving at the metal. He pushed and pushed and pushed, but nothing moved. "Are you just going to stand there, or are you going to help me?" he finally asked.

"That's not going to work," I told him calmly. "See that big button up there?" I pointed to a panel

by the sign. "I think it's an automatic door. Someone has to push that button for us to get through."

Accessable

UP
△
▽
DOWN

"Okay, I'll do it!" he shouted again, and he started
jumping up and down in the air trying to reach the button.

I couldn't help myself, I just started laughing. Here was this tiny kitten, trying to jump four feet into the air and then push a giant button. "Rev," I giggled, "I can't even reach that, let alone you!"

He stopped jumping and turned to look at me. "Then what do we do?"

"We have to wait for a person to either go in or out, then we go through."

"Okay."

So we stood there in the middle of the hallway, trying to look casual so no one would notice us.

We jumped when we heard a loud, "BING," and the door slid open.

"Hurry!" I told him.

We ran past the people coming out and went in the door, but once inside, we realized that this room didn't go anywhere! It was only about four feet square with no way out except for the door we had just come through. And that door closed behind us.

"What now?" Rev asked.

I shrugged. "Wait for the door to open again, I guess."

The person who was in the room with us was pushing buttons on the wall. That was weird. I had never seen a bunch of buttons on the wall like that. Then the floor started to move!

"CHARLIE!" Rev screeched, and the person turned to look at us.

"What are you cats doing in the elevator?" he asked.

"Meow," I answered.

"Maybe I need to ask them to check my medication," the man said as the door opened, and he walked out.

It closed again before we got through. That was when I noticed the numbers next to the buttons on the wall. The numbers were the same as the ones I had seen on the sign outside the door. Maybe if we went to the number that was marked for "CHILDREN'S WARD," we would be in the right place.

"We're going to have to stay in here until someone pushes the number 6 up there," I told Rev.

"But Charlie, this room moves! Rooms aren't supposed to do that!"

"Well, I guess this one is. We need to stand here in the back, quietly, until someone pushes the right number, then we can leave and find Jeffery."

"Are you sure?"

"No, but it's the only thing that makes sense," I answered.

"Moving rooms make sense to you? Wow, you really must be smart."

Smart or not, I thought I was going to be sick before someone pushed the number 6. Five times people got in and out of that tiny room, and five times my stomach went up and down. Sometimes the room would move all by itself, with nobody in there, and then the door would open and a person would enter.

Creepy.

Finally, a lady stepped in with a little girl holding her hand. "You can only visit your brother for a few minutes," she was saying. "He gets to come home with us tomorrow, so the nurse said it would be okay for you to see him." She pushed the number 6.

"All right Rev, get ready," I whispered.

The little girl turned and looked at us. "Mommy, why are there kitties in the elevator?" she asked.

"Hmm?" the mom said, watching the lights at the top of the door.

"I said, why are there cats in the elevator?"

"There are no cats in the hospital honey, they're not allowed," the mom answered as the doors opened, and she pulled the girl out of the elevator.

"But Mommy…" she was saying as she was led away.

I winked at her before she disappeared from sight, and Rev and I raced out of the little room and jumped behind a garbage can.

It was another big room. There was a square area in the middle, with nurses standing there watching computer screens and writing on papers. Every few minutes, people would walk up to them and ask where to find someone. The nurses would look on a piece of paper and then tell the person the patients room number.

"We need to get a look at that list," I told Rev.

"How do we do that, Charlie? You heard what that lady said, cats aren't allowed in here. If anyone sees us, they'll throw us out."

"Let me think a minute," I said.

I continued to watch the nurses. They were all working very hard going from room to room and then coming back to the central area. If only they would all leave at the same time….

"We need a distraction," I told Rev. "Something to get the nurses attention. If you can think of something that will make them all step away for a moment, I can run over, read the paper, and find out what room Jeffery is in. Any ideas?"

Rev looked around. "I can hear kids playing down the hall," he said. "Let's go check it out. Maybe there's something there we can use."

We carefully made our way down the long, white hall to another big, open room. This one was painted with cartoon characters on the walls, and there were toys all around. Five kids were in the room, all wearing funny pajamas, and they seemed to be playing very carefully with the toys.

Over in one corner, a young boy was playing with blocks. He was stacking them up higher and higher, creating a structure almost as tall as he was. It had worked for me once before, maybe it would work again....

"Rev, see that boy over there? I'm going to go back down the hall to the desk area. Give me about two minutes to get there. Then I want you to run over, knock that building down, and then hide before anyone sees you. Got it?"

"I got it, but won't the boy see me?"

"Yeah, but if you hide fast enough, it will be just like the girl in the elevator. None of the adults will believe there's really a cat here unless they see it themselves."

"Okay, I'll be ready!" He slunk over to a chair right by the blocks.

I made my way quickly back down the hall, until I could hide myself right by the counter where the nurses were working. Then I waited.

Seconds later, a huge crash sounded from the playroom. "What was that?" I heard one of the nurse's shout, and they all ran to see what had happened.

I jumped up onto the counter and ran over to the paper I had seen the nurses looking at. It was a list of all the children on this floor and what room number they were in. Perfect. I found Jeffery's name, then dove back down and hid before the nurses returned.

"Can you believe that kid?" One of the nurses was asking. "Makes a huge mess in there and then tries to blame it on a cat. When I ask him where the cat was, he says it must have gone invisible. Kids. You gotta love 'em."

I made my way to the playroom. Rev was again hiding behind the same chair, a big smile on his face. "That was fun!"

"It worked, too. I've got the number, let's go find Jeffery's room."

Chapter 11

Cat's Don't Make Me Sick

THERE WERE two beds in Jeffery's room. A boy even younger than Andrew was sleeping in the first one; Jeffery was laying on the other, staring out the window. He looked a little younger than Amanda, with dark hair and big brown eyes. He had a tube coming out of one of his arms, going up to this big bag full of what looked like water. He had a little plastic thing clipped to one of the fingers on his other hand. It was hooked up to this small TV thing that beeped and showed a jagged green line. Around his face, he had a tiny mask, but it only went over his nose, not over his eyes like a disguise would. He looked small and weak. I could only imagine how Rev was feeling. I would never want to see one of my family like that.

81

I looked at Rev, but instead of being scared, his face was shining with happiness. "It's him!"

He ran over to the bed and tried to jump up. Jeffery hadn't noticed him yet, and Rev was way too small to leap that high. "Charlie, help me!" he cried.

I wasn't sure how I could get him that high. It was too far up for him to just climb over me, and not having hands, I couldn't jump up myself and then pull him after me. I needed to somehow help him leap higher.

I smiled.

Rev continued to jump, over and over again, trying to catch ahold of the sheets and pull himself up. On one of these leaps, I got underneath him and clawed him in the rear.

"OUCH!" he screamed, but it made him pounce about a foot higher, and he got his claws into the bottom of the mattress. I reached up on my hind legs and pushed on his tail end until he pulled himself the rest of the way. "Why did you do that?" he turned and asked me angrily.

"Look where you are," I answered calmly.

He turned and saw that he was right next to his boy. Jeffery had turned from the window when he heard Rev screech, and was just staring in wonder at his kitten. "Rev? How did you get here?" he exclaimed with joy as he hugged him.

I leapt up next to them on the bed. Rev stopped

rubbing up against Jeffery long enough to come over and smile at me, rub his head against my chest, and then walk back to his boy.

Jeffery looked at me. "I know you, you're Charlie! You live at Amanda and Andrew's house. Did you help Rev get here?" he asked. In answer, Rev started his loud purring, and Jeffery just smiled. "Thanks Charlie. I feel better just knowing he's here with me." He reached over and started petting me, too.

We both snuggled up against Jeffery, one of us on either side of him, and began to relax. It had been quite an adventure getting there, and as Jeffery began telling Rev everything that had been happening to him, from getting to the hospital all the way to what terrible food they served, I felt myself falling asleep.

I don't know how long I napped, but I suddenly felt the sheet being pulled up over my head and realized that something was going on. Someone had come into the room, and Jeffery had pulled the blankets up over both Rev and me to keep us from being spotted. Smart kid.

"How are you feeling Jeffery?" I heard his mom's voice ask.

"Much better now mom. Guess what happened?"

"Why don't you tell me later honey? The doctor is here, and he wants to talk with us."

"I have good news and bad news Jeffery," I heard a mans voice say. "The good news is, you get to go home today."

"Yes!" Jeffery shouted.

"Your virus is gone, so you are breathing well again. But, we're worried about what will happen when you get home. We know you've been sick before, and we want to get rid of anything that could be a problem in the future. That way, you won't have to come back to the hospital." He paused for a moment.

"Yeah, I don't want to have to come back here ever again," Jeffery agreed.

"Jeffery, one of the things that can cause problems for a lot of kids is pet fur. Usually, if we make sure there are no pets in a house, it makes it so the children don't have trouble breathing anymore."

I felt Jeffery's body get very tense, and he turned his head toward his mom. "What's he talking about? He doesn't mean what I think he means, does he?"

"Yes honey, I'm afraid he does," his mom answered. "I'm sorry, but we're going to have to find a new home for Rev."

I looked over Jeffery's chest, to where Rev was laying against him. Rev's eyes were huge, and he looked as if he were about to cry.

Then I felt Jeffery's arms tighten around both of us. "Doctor, you just said I'm doing much better now, right?"

"Yes. You're doing even better now than you were just a few hours ago."

"And you think it's because I'm here in the hospital?"

"No. The main reason you're better is because

the virus you had is gone, but we think you are breathing better because you're away from any fur."

"So, you think if I were around my cat, that I would start feeling bad again?" Jeffery asked.

"I think so. That's why we needed to talk to you about him. We think you will stay healthy if you stay away from Rev."

"But you say I'm healthy now, right?" he pushed.

"Yes. You are doing really well right now."

"Then my cat is not the problem."

"Why do you think that, Jeffery?" his mom asked.

"This is why!" he shouted as he yanked back the covers to reveal Rev and I, all snuggled up against him.

We smiled up at the doctor.

He jumped three feet away from the bed in shock. "How did those cats get here?" he asked.

"I don't know, but I'm feeling better now than I have since I got here, so it's definitely not cats that make me feel bad. They make me feel good."

"But," the doctor started.

"Doctor," Jeffery's mom interrupted. "I think you need to figure out what's actually causing my son's problems, because he just proved that you are wrong."

The doctor looked uncomfortable. "We'll run a few more tests before he leaves today, to see if we can find anything else." He started walking toward the door. "I'll have someone come in and take those cats out of the hospital."

"Oh no you won't," Jeffery's mom stated. "Obviously, they help Jeffery to feel better. If he's only going to be here for a few more hours, and he has to take more tests in the meantime, then I think they can stay here and keep him company."

"It's against hospital policy...."

"It's against hospital policy for them to be here, but somehow they got in anyway. I have a friend who works for the local newspaper. I bet she would be interested in a story about how two cats managed to get past hospital security and make it all the way to the sixth floor...."

"All right, they can stay," the doctor agreed. "But make sure they remain on the bed with Jeffery the entire time. We don't need them out wandering the halls."

Been there, done that.

Rev and I smiled at each other as the doctor walked out the door. As soon as he was gone, Jeffery's mom got on the phone. I thought she was going to call the newspaper like she had threatened, but she was actually calling my house.

"Hi, it's me. You're not going to believe who came to the hospital to visit Jeffery...."

We spent the whole afternoon lying on a bed, getting stroked by everyone who came in the room. The nurses who heard about us all came in to look, and they brought treats from other people's lunch plates as a snack. Who said hospitals aren't fun? Rev and I had a great time!

When all the tests were done, Jeffery got dressed, and the three of us got to ride down to the front of the hospital in a wheelchair. People stared at us in the halls and on the elevators, but we just smiled and pretended there was nothing unusual about two cats riding around a medical facility with a little boy.

Unfortunately, we had to ride home in a car. Again. I hate cars.

They dropped me off at home, where I had to say "goodbye." Rev was curled up on Jeffery's lap making that super loud purring noise. He looked at me with a tear in those big eyes of his. "Charlie, you are the bravest cat on the planet. Thank you for helping me get my boy back."

I smiled. "You take good care of him, and maybe he'll bring you back to visit sometime."

A huge smile broke out across his face. "Yeah, that would be great!"

Amanda was waiting for me. She picked me up and hugged me tightly. "Charlie, how do you always manage to get yourself so far from home?" she asked.

Trust me, it's not my idea, I thought. If I never have to leave my neighborhood again, I will be one happy cat.

Chapter 12

The Return of Boredom

HAVE YOU ever noticed that every time life gets to be just the way you like it, just the way you pictured it should be, it can get really boring?

Somehow, things just weren't the same without that crazy kitten running around getting into everything. I tried to spice things up myself; I chased Rose around the house while she was in her ball (she yelled at me), I played with Frisky's tail (she almost bit me), I even tried throwing around a piece of dog food (I almost threw up when I tasted it). Nothing seemed to brighten my mood. It just felt like something was missing.

A few days later, I was taking a nap in the bathtub. This may sound strange to you, but I live in Arizona where the weather gets really warm, and the bathtub stays nice and cool. I was just starting to really drift off into a good dream. I was a lion, creeping through the jungle, looking for my prey. Sneaking between the trees, I looked through the bushes and spotted a gazelle. It was just standing there, as if waiting to be my next victim. I knew I had to stay silent until I was close enough to strike....

"CHARLIE!"

I jumped three feet in the air and hit my head on the faucet. Rubbing it gently with my paw, I turned to growl at whoever had so rudely awoken me.

"Hi Charlie! How are you? Were you taking a nap?"

Rev asked. He had jumped up on the edge of the bathtub and was balancing precariously on the side.

"Uh, yeah. Obviously," I said as I continued rubbing the bump that was forming on my forehead. "What are you doing here?"

"Well, it turns out Jeffery has some weird allergy thing, and he has to go to another city for treatment. So every two weeks, I get to come and spend the weekend with you, while he and his parents are out of town. Isn't that great?"

I almost said something sarcastic, as I wasn't really thrilled to see him at the moment. Then I thought about how boring things had been around the house for the last few days. "Yeah, that's great, Rev." I stopped rubbing my head and reached up to pat his. After giving him a big brotherly rub on the shoulder, I tapped his paw a little harder. "Tag," I said. "You're it!" I jumped out of the bathtub and raced from the room.

I ran down the hall slowly, making sure he was right behind me. I knew those little legs of his couldn't keep up with mine, so I didn't turn on full speed. As we reached the living room, just as he thought he was about to catch me, I leaped up over the back of the sofa, clearing it and landing on the floor on the other side.

"No way!" I could hear him yell. "It was way cool, but that's cheating!"

"I don't think so. It's not my fault you can't do that." I was so busy sitting there feeling smug about how cool I was, that I didn't notice Rev sneak around the corner of the couch.

"Tag!" he said as he hit my paw. He was so excited to have gotten me that he jumped a foot straight up in the air, turning around as he leapt, and landed on the ground running the other way.

Not bad.

We chased each other through the house for the next hour. Mom yelled at us twice, Amanda almost tripped over us running past her, and Andrew got used as a hurdle several times, before we finally wore each other out and decided to take a nap. We snuggled up together in a chair like the buddies we'd become, and I fell asleep almost as fast as Rev did.

I was back in the jungle again, getting closer and closer to my prey. I could smell the green leaves on the moist, hot air, and my whiskers prickled as I reached out with all of my senses for the slightest movement of the gazelle, when suddenly....

"Wev, stop it."

"Wev, stop it!"

"WEV, STOP IT!"

I was a little irate at being woken up from my dream again before I had even gotten close enough for a good pounce. Rev was no longer asleep next to me, and Andrew was obviously not happy with him, so I went into the front room to see what the problem was.

Andrew was sitting in a recliner playing video games. He was holding the controller in his hands and concentrating very hard on the screen. Rev was sitting behind him, up on the back of the chair, staring out the window. He was watching something that had him very excited. I could tell, because his tail was twitching back and forth, back and forth. Every time it swung to the right, his tail hit Andrew in the face.

"Wev, cut it out!" he yelled again.

"Hey, Rev," I called. "You're driving Andrew crazy. What are you doing?"

"There's a bird right out there!" Rev whispered. His whole body went totally still, and then he slowly lowered himself down on his legs.

I knew what was coming. "No Rev, don't do it!"

BAM! I was too late. In his excitement over the bird, Rev had launched himself straight into the window.

"Ouch!" He found himself lying on the floor, rubbing a bump on his head. I walked up to him shaking my head. Kittens.

"Not very smart, huh?" he asked me.

I smiled at him. "Don't feel too bad. I've done the same thing at least twice because of that stupid bird. He lives in the cactus right outside the window."

"Well, maybe we should figure out a way to evict him from his home then," Rev answered. He smiled a vicious smile. "Make him move right into my tummy!" he giggled.

Having Rev around every two weeks was going to be fun. I was glad he got Jeffery back and would be living with his family; he had way too much energy to live with all the time. But having him around to play with once in awhile would be a real blast.

"Rev," I told him. "Let me explain to you about the terrible taste of feathers…."

Don't miss any of Charlie's Great Adventures!

And coming soon...

Charlie the Spy

C.A. Goody loves to hear from her readers. You can send her an e-mail through her website:

www.charliethecat.com